Alfred A. Knopf
New York

THE
START

KIT FEENY:
ON THE MOVE

Alfred A. Knopf
New York

THIS IS A BORZOI BOOK PUBLISHED BY ALFRED A. KNOPF

This is a work of fiction. Names, characters, places, and incidents either are the product of the author's imagination or are used fictitiously. Any resemblance to actual persons, living or dead, events, or locales is entirely coincidental.

Copyright © 2009 by Michael Townsend

All rights reserved. Published in the United States by Alfred A. Knopf, an imprint of Random House Children's Books, a division of Random House, Inc., New York.

Knopf, Borzoi Books, and the colophon are registered trademarks of Random House, Inc.

Visit us on the Web! www.randomhouse.com/kids

Educators and librarians, for a variety of teaching tools, visit us at www.randomhouse.com/teachers

Library of Congress Cataloging-in-Publication Data
Townsend, Michael.
Kit Feeny: On the Move / Michael Townsend. — 1st ed.
p.   cm. — (Kit Feeny ; #1)
Summary: When plucky Kit Feeny moves to a new town, he immediately makes an enemy of the school bully and must struggle to find a new best friend who shares his interests.
ISBN 978-0-375-85614-3 (trade) — ISBN 978-0-375-95614-0 (lib. bdg.)
1. Graphic novels. [1. Graphic novels. 2. Moving, Household—Fiction. 3. Friendship—Fiction. 4. Bullies—Fiction.]
I. Title.
PZ7.7.T69Ki 2009
741.5'973—dc22
2008037443

MAR   2011

Pen and Ink Drawings With Digital Coloring
MANUFACTURED IN MALAYSIA
October 2009
10 9 8 7 6 5 4 3 2
First Edition
Random House Children's Books supports the First Amendment and celebrates the right to read.

CHICKENS

MRS. FEENY

MR. FEENY

COWS

TABLE OF CONTENTS

ARNOLD

APRIL FEENY

BONNIE FEENY

KIT FEENY

PART 1.
THE MYSTERY
BOX

TODAY WAS MOVING DAY FOR KIT FEENY.

GOODBYE, OLD HOUSE!

SOLD

IT WAS A MORNING FILLED WITH COUNTLESS SAD GOODBYES TO THE OLD AND FAMILIAR...

GOODBYE, COWS!

GOODBYE, CHICKENS!

AND AN AFTERNOON OF MANY AWKWARD HELLOS TO THE NEW AND STRANGE.

HELLO, MINI-COW!

HELLO, STRANGE-LOOKING CHICKENS!

WE'RE HERE!

HELLO, NEW HOUSE!

A SHORT TIME LATER, AFTER A LONG TALKING-TO...

BLAH BLAH BLAH **DANGEROUS** BLAH BLAH BLAH BLAH BLAH **IRRESPONSIBLE** BLAH BLAH BLAH BLAH BLAH BLAH BLAH BLAH BLAH **JAIL** BLAH BLAH BLAH BLAH BLAH BLAH

ARRANGEMENTS WERE MADE TO SEND ARNOLD BACK HOME.

I JUST GOT OFF THE PHONE WITH YOUR PARENTS. WE'RE GOING TO MEET THEM HALFWAY.

WE SHOULD HAVE PUT A TOILET IN THE BOX.

TOTALLY.

YOU CAN RIDE IN THE CAR THIS TIME, ARNOLD.

OH. RIGHT.

KIT WAS ABOUT TO PROTEST, BUT HE REALIZED NOW WAS NOT THE TIME. BESIDES, HE REALLY DID NEED NEW CLOTHES, THANKS TO A POORLY EXECUTED PLAN FROM EARLIER THAT SUMMER.

IT HAD STARTED OUT SIMPLY ENOUGH.

KIT AND ARNOLD TOOK ALL THEIR MONEY TO GO BUY SOME PIZZA.

BUT ON THE WAY TO THE PIZZA SHOP...

THEY SAW A TOY STORE AND SPENT ALL THEIR MONEY ON BOUNCY BALLS...

AND QUICKLY LOST ALL 1,000.

EXHAUSTED AND STILL HUNGRY, THEY REALIZED THEY HAD A PROBLEM.

SO KIT CAME UP WITH A BRILLIANT PLAN: OPERATION PIZZA MONEY!

THE BOYS PAINTED PICTURES ON ALL THEIR CLOTHES
AND SOLD THEM TO THEIR FRIENDS.

BUSINESS WAS GREAT! THEY SOLD EVERY LAST PIECE OF CLOTHING THEY HAD, EXCEPT WHAT THEY WERE WEARING.

THIS TIME WHEN THEY WENT TO BUY PIZZA, THEY WERE EXTRA CAREFUL TO AVOID LOOKING AT THE TOY STORE.

THINGS WERE GOING GREAT UNTIL...

THEIR MOTHERS FOUND OUT WHAT THEY HAD DONE.
THE BEST FRIENDS WERE IN BIG TROUBLE!

THEIR PUNISHMENTS INCLUDED A LONG GROUNDING...AND THEY HAD
TO WEAR THE ONLY OUTFITS THEY HAD LEFT...

FOR THE REST OF THE SUMMER.

THIS WAS THE BEST PART OF THE PUNISHMENT!

AS THE FEENYS MADE THEIR WAY TO THE MALL, KIT SCRIBBLED IN HIS SKETCHBOOK, HOPING IT MIGHT HELP KEEP HIS MIND OFF ARNOLD.

BUT NO MATTER HOW MANY WARTS AND HORNS HE ADDED TO HIS SISTERS' PICTURE, HIS MIND WAS STILL ON HIS BEST FRIEND.

PART 2.
THE SHIRT OF WONDER

WHEN THE FEENYS ARRIVED AT THE MALL, THE GIRLS WERE OVERWHELMED. THEY HAD NEVER SEEN SUCH A LARGE SELECTION OF CLOTHES!

PANT PANT PANT THE GIRLS BACK HOME WOULD BE SOOO JEALOUS!

I'M SOOO HAPPY!

THIS IS A BEAUTIFUL GIRL'S PARADISE!

SHOPPING SHOPPING SHOPPING

GIRLS, STOP MAKING A SCENE!

AND...HEY, WHERE'D KIT GO?

KIT?

HEY, BONNIE, SHOULD WE FEEL GUILTY FOR LOOKING SO PRETTY?

ARE PONIES STUPID?

NO!

KIT?

NOW LET'S GO FIND YOU SOME ADORABLE PUMPKIN CLOTHES.

AT FIRST, KIT DIDN'T SEE A SINGLE THING HE LIKED.

GOODY!

HMMM...HERE'S SOMETHING.

GROAN

BEEP BEEP BEEP

WHAT WAS ALL THAT BEEPING? YOU ASK. OH, IT'S JUST MY UGLY-METER GOING OFF!

WELL, HOW ABOUT THIS? ALL THE KIDS ARE WEARING IT. IT'S THE BEE'S KNEES.

EEP BEEP BEEP

WHAT DO YOU THINK?

YOU LOOK ADORABLE. WE'LL TAKE IT!

FAB-U-LOUS.

BUT YOU STILL NEED SOME OTHER OUTFITS.

BEEP BEEP AND BEEP

I ONLY WANT MORE CLOTHES JUST LIKE THIS—

AWESOME AND STUPID!

LOOK HOW HAPPY HE IS!

I'M HAPPY THAT HE'S HAPPY.

KIT FORGOT ABOUT HIS PROBLEMS AND JOINED IN THE FUN...

UNTIL...

WOW! I BET ARNOLD WOULD HAVE LOVED THAT SHIRT!

EEEP

GOOD NIGHT, EVERYBODY. I'M GOING TO MY NEW ROOM TO UNPACK.

OOOPS

MY PAL

I CAN'T BELIEVE I ALMOST FORGOT ABOUT YOU, BEST FRIEND!!!

WE LOVE GUMMY FISH...

SO WE DECIDED TO MAKE THEM OURSELVES. BUT WE DIDN'T KNOW HOW.

SO WE THOUGHT... AND THOUGHT...

UNTIL OUR HEADS HURT.

THEN—BOOM—IT HIT US!

BOOM

ARNOLD GOT A PACKET OF JELL-O ™...

JELL-O

AND I BORROWED MY SISTERS' GOLDFISH.

MR. FISH-FISH

THEN WE TRIED TO GET MR. FISH-FISH TO EAT THE JELL-O ™ GOODNESS.

JELL-O

EAT EAT EAT

EAT EAT EAT

MR. FISH-FISH DIDN'T SEEM TO CARE FOR THE POWDER.

MAYBE WE SHOULD STIR IT!

THIS SAYS WE'RE SUPPOSED TO REFRIGERATE IT!

JELLO

SO WE DID. THEN WE WAITED.

LA LA LA

IT WAS A FAILURE.

OOOOOPS

AND MR. FISH-FISH DIED...

SO WE FLUSHED HIM.

BUT THE TOILET CLOGGED.

MOM GOT REALLY, REALLY MAD!!!

DAD HAD TO GO TO THE PET STORE...

GRRRR

TO GET A NEW MR. FISH-FISH.

THE STUPID GIRLS NEVER KNEW...

BUT WE STILL GOT GROUNDED FOR A WEEK.

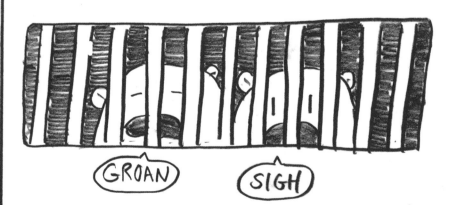

THE SAD BUT TRUE END.

PART 3.
THE NOT-SO-GREAT FIRST DAY

I'M SO EXCITED, APRIL!

ME TOO, BONNIE! WE'RE GOING TO MAKE SO MANY NEW FRIENDS TODAY!

WELL, I'M NOT!

HUH?!

I'M ONLY GOING TO MAKE ONE NEW FRIEND—

A REPLACEMENT ARNOLD!

HEE HEE HEE HA HA HA HA HE HA HE HA HA HA

LAUGH ALL YOU WANT...

BUT IT'S A REPLACEMENT ARNOLD OR NOTHING!

TO HELP ME ON MY QUEST, I'VE MADE SEVERAL FANTASTIC TESTS.

ARNOLD TEST!!!

HEE HEE HEE

OUR GOOFY BROTHER MADE "ARNOLD TESTS"!

HERE'S THE BUS STOP!

HEY, NEW KID.

YEAH?

YOU BETTER MOVE, AND QUICK, 'CAUSE YOU'RE IN DEVON THE BULLY COMEDIAN'S SEAT!

SO?

SO, I'M A LAUGH RIOT!!! BUT WHO ARE YOU, AND WHAT ARE YOU DOING IN MY SEAT?

UM...I'M KIT FEENY. I'M NEW AND I DIDN'T KNOW THIS WAS YOUR SEAT.

OH YEAH? WELL, YOUR FACE NEEDS WORK! HA HA HA

A FEW MOMENTS LATER KIT MET HIS NEW PRINCIPAL.

LOOKS LIKE WE HAVE A TROUBLED ARTIST ON OUR HANDS HERE.

BUT BEFORE I PUNISH YOU, MIT, THERE'S SOMETHING YOU SHOULD KNOW.

MY NAME'S KIT!

OF COURSE IT IS!

BESIDES BEING AN AWARD-WINNING PRINCIPAL...

I'M ALSO AN AWARD-WINNING ARTIST!

THIS IS A PAIR OF POO-POO WOMPS THAT I PAINTED.

IT WON A BLUE RIBBON AT THE COUNTY FAIR!

WHAT DO YOU THINK, MIT?

MY NAME'S NOT—

SAY! I HAVE AN IDEA! HOW ABOUT INSTEAD OF DRAWING MEAN PICTURES...

FROM NOW ON YOU ONLY DRAW HAPPY PICTURES? THEN MAYBE SOMEDAY YOU MIGHT END UP LIKE ME!!!

INSTEAD OF IN JAIL!

AS KIT WALKED, SOMETHING THE PRINCIPAL SAID KEPT REPEATING IN HIS HEAD.

EACH BIRD IS SPECIAL IN ITS OWN WAY!

AND THAT IS HOW KIT FIGURED OUT THAT...

ARNOLD CAN NEVER BE REPLACED!

IF...IF...I CAN'T HAVE THE ORIGINAL ARNOLD...

AND HE CAN'T BE REPLACED WITH A DUPLICATE...

THEN... THEN...

PART 4.
KIT FEENY IS THE LONESOME HOBO

WHEN KIT RETURNED HOME, HE WAS READY TO BEGIN HIS NEW LIFE.

WHERE WERE YOU?

WE SAVED YOU A SEAT WITH US.

HEY, WHAT ARE YOU DOING?

I'M PACKING.

PACKING FOR WHAT?

FOR MY NEW LIFE AS A HOBO.

OUR BROTHER IS A LOONY-NUT!

YEAH... I THINK I'LL DO THAT.

SON, WON'T YOU BE LONELY AS A LONELY HOBO?

THAT'S THE WHOLE POINT, DAD!

BBRRRRRRRRR

BUT I MIGHT EVENTUALLY GET A DOG.

I'LL NAME HIM ARNOLD. BUT NOT BECAUSE I'M REPLACING THE REAL ARNOLD.

BING

BECAUSE THAT IS IMPOSSIBLE.

BEANS

MUNCH

MUNCH

MUNCH

MUNCH

NCH

HE DECIDED TO END HIS LIFE AS A HOBO.

A SHORT TIME LATER KIT AND MRS. FEENY HAD A PACKAGE OF WONDER READY TO GO!

OKAY, ALL DONE. I'LL MAIL IT TOMORROW! BY THE WAY, WHAT DID YOUR NOTE SAY?

THAT I DON'T WANT HIM TO BECOME A LONELY HOBO!

SO HE SHOULD MAKE LOTS OF GREAT NEW FRIENDS, BUT NOT REPLACEMENT KITS.

ARE YOU GOING TO TAKE YOUR OWN ADVICE?

YEAH... I GUESS.

DO YOU HAVE ANYBODY IN MIND?

THERE WAS THIS ONE GUY, BUT HE DIDN'T KNOW ABOUT GRAPHIC NOVELS.

WELL, WHY DON'T YOU TEACH HIM?

THAT'S A GREAT IDEA!

KIT RACED TO HIS NEW ROOM AND CAREFULLY PICKED OUT SOME OF HIS FAVORITE GRAPHIC NOVELS. HE WAS EXCITED TO SHOW THEM TO HIS POSSIBLE NEW BEST FRIEND, BUT...

HMMMM

AS HE FLIPPED THROUGH THEM...

HE WAS REMINDED OF A CERTAIN COMEDIAN FROM EARLIER THAT DAY.

HAHAHA

WAIT A SECOND!

WHO WILL WANT TO BE FRIENDS WITH A BULLY'S FAVORITE TARGET?

I NEED TO SOLVE MY DEVON PROBLEM FIRST!

KIT BEGAN TO THINK REALLY, REALLY, REALLY HARD.

HUMUNA HUMUNA

THINK

THINK

THINK

PLUNGE PLUNGE PLUNGE

I NEED AN IDEA, SCARY STUFFED CLOWN!

HMMMM...

HUZZAH! I GOT ONE!

IT MIGHT ACTUALLY WORK!

KIT QUICKLY GRABBED A FLASHLIGHT AND SOME WRITING STUFF...

AND WENT INTO HIS LITTLE CLOSET...

WHERE HE WORKED HARD LATE INTO THE NIGHT.

IF YOU THINK IT'S WEIRD TO WORK IN A CLOSET, IT'S PROBABLY BECAUSE YOU NEVER TRIED IT.

PART 5.
OPERATION: I HOPE THIS WORKS

AFTER BREAKFAST, KIT NERVOUSLY HEADED OFF TO THE BUS STOP.

BYE, MY HONEY BUNNIES!

GOOD LUCK, SPORT!

HEY, MOM?

WHAT IS IT, GIRLS?

IF KIT DECIDES TO BE A HOBO AGAIN TODAY...

CAN WE HAVE HIS ROOM?

PLEASE!

GO TO SCHOOL, GIRLS.

GOODBYE, MY LOVELY-SMELLING BABIES.

BYE, OUR BEAUTIFUL MOMMY.

AS KIT BRAVELY APPROACHED THE BUS STOP, WHAT HE SAW SHOCKED HIM.

HIYA, KIT!

URP

I HOPE YOU DON'T MIND— MY MOM TOOK ME TO THE MALL AND GOT ME THIS SHIRT!

NO, I DON'T MIND.

EEEP

URP

BUT AREN'T YOU AFRAID OF GETTING PICKED ON LIKE I WAS?

HEY, MAN, THESE SHIRTS ARE AWESOME. I JUST HOPE I DON'T GET BLOOD ON IT IF DEVON PUNCHES ME!

COOL! AND I BROUGHT YOU SOME OF MY FAVORITE GRAPHIC NOVELS!

THOSE ARE COMIC BOOKS!

I LOVE COMICS!

IS THAT THE NEW ISSUE OF *ELEPHANT GONE CRAZY?*

YOU KNOW IT!

ELEPHANT GONE CRAZY #17

KIT WAS ABOUT TO FIND OUT AS DEVON THE BULLY COMEDIAN STOMPED ONTO THE BUS.

HOLY McFART-AGAIN! THERE'S TWO OF THEM!

THIS IS GOING TO BE SOOOOOO MUCH FUN.

FIRST I'M GOING TO MOCK THEM TILL THEY CRY. THEN I'M GOING TO BEAT THEIR EYES SHUT TILL THEY STOP CRYING.

OKAY, BUT BEFORE YOU DO THAT...

COULD YOU READ THIS?

A FEW MINUTES LATER AT SCHOOL.

THANKS AGAIN FOR THOSE JOKES!

YOU'RE WELCOME.

CAN YOU GET ME SOME MORE?

NO.

GRRRR. WELL, IF YOU DON'T...

HANG ON THERE, DEVON.

I WON'T WRITE YOU ANY MORE, BUT I WILL TRY AND HELP YOU WRITE YOUR OWN.

REALLY?

JUST TWO RULES:

1. YOU GOTTA STOP BEATING UP PEOPLE, AND

2. WHATEVER JOKES WE WRITE WON'T BE TOO MEAN.

SURE! THAT SOUNDS GREAT!

LET'S MEET UP AT RECESS.

PART 6.
THE NEW MYSTERY BOX

OVER THE NEXT FEW WEEKS, KIT'S NEW FRIENDSHIP WITH HOFF GREW BY LEAPS AND BOUNDS.

WOW! LOOK AT MR. FROGGY JUMP!

TIME TO RUN, KIT.

EEEEKK

ICKY

I AGREE!

THINGS WERE GOOD WITH DEVON THE COMEDIAN TOO.

HEY, PLANT, DID YOU JUST GET OFF A BOAT?

NO, WHY DO YOU ASK?

'CAUSE YOU'RE ALL GREEN, LIKE YOU'RE SEASICK!

HA HA HA

GROAN

HEE

HE STILL NEEDS SOME WORK.

THEN ONE DAY AFTER SCHOOL, KIT GOT A PACKAGE IN THE MAIL.

OH BOY, OH BOY!

RIIIIPP

WHO SENT IT?

IT'S FROM MY FIRST BEST FRIEND!

TO KIT

THE
END